Vegetable
Gardens

River Bièvre

Dye
Works

Weaving
Workshop

Thérèse's
Home

Courtyard

S

E   W

N

Painting
Studio

Avenue des Gobelins

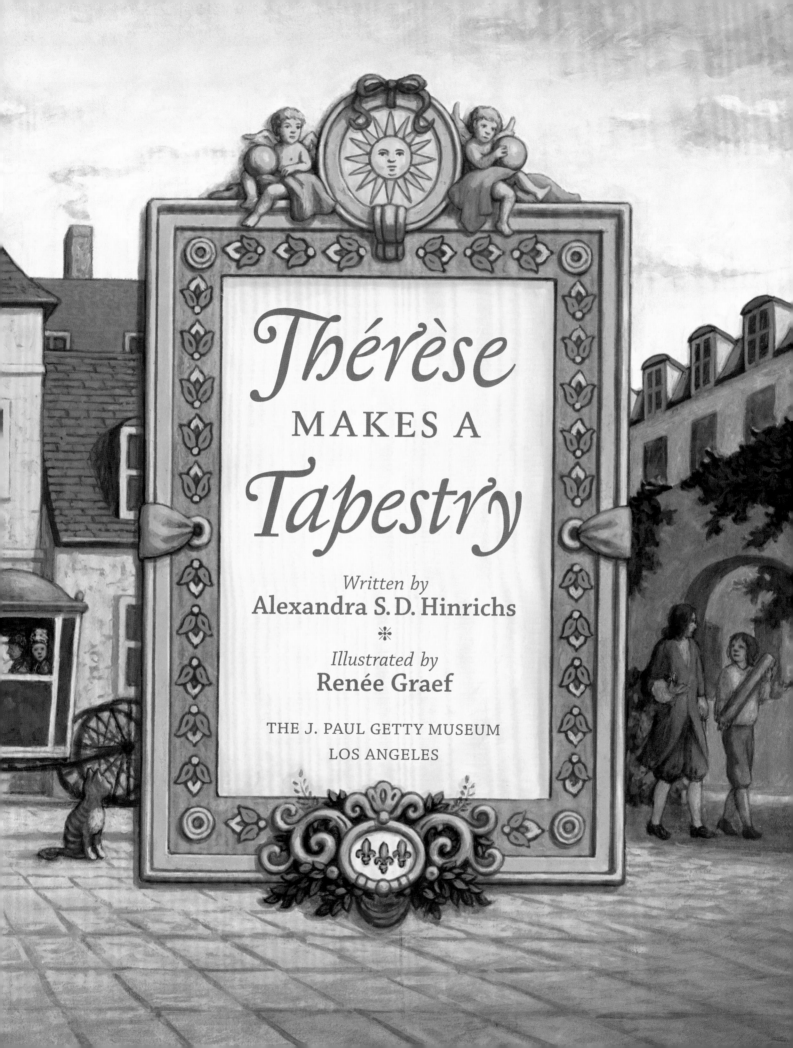

Thérèse
MAKES A
Tapestry

Written by
Alexandra S. D. Hinrichs

✳

Illustrated by
Renée Graef

THE J. PAUL GETTY MUSEUM
LOS ANGELES

hérèse ran her fingers over the soft wool yarn, the finest in all of Paris. The weaving workshop breathed around her. Swish. Creak. Clank. Whir. Swish. These were the sounds of home. Thérèse was the daughter, granddaughter, and great-granddaughter of weavers and painters. Papa liked to joke that their family was made of yarn and paintbrushes instead of skin and bones.

Thérèse and her parents and brothers worked for King Louis XIV in the Gobelins Manufactory, where they made tapestries destined for the walls of splendid palaces. Thérèse and her mother used

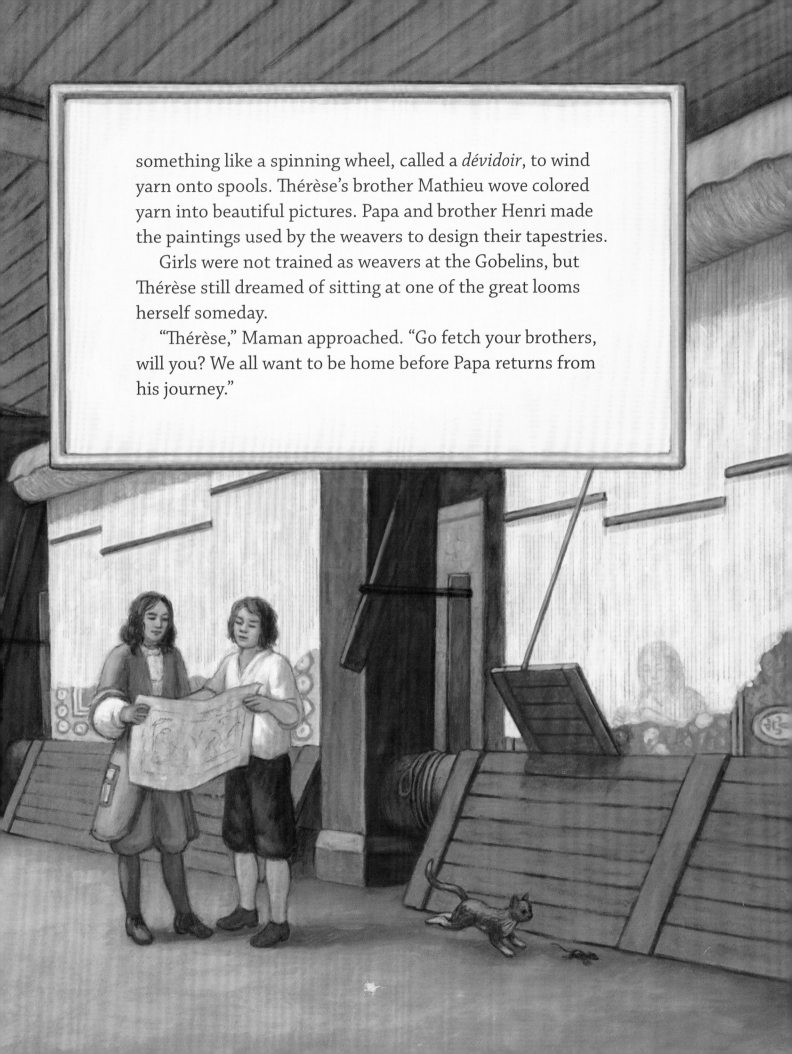

something like a spinning wheel, called a *dévidoir*, to wind yarn onto spools. Thérèse's brother Mathieu wove colored yarn into beautiful pictures. Papa and brother Henri made the paintings used by the weavers to design their tapestries.

Girls were not trained as weavers at the Gobelins, but Thérèse still dreamed of sitting at one of the great looms herself someday.

"Thérèse," Maman approached. "Go fetch your brothers, will you? We all want to be home before Papa returns from his journey."

As she neared Mathieu's loom, Thérèse could see his hands darting in and out of the yarns that stretched from the top to the bottom. Suddenly he popped his face through and startled her. "Do you have a message for me, little bird?"

Thérèse laughed. "It's time to go. Papa is coming tonight!"

They went to the painting studio, where their brother Henri was cleaning his brushes. Henri was older and more serious than Mathieu, but even he couldn't hide his excitement about Papa's return. They all hurried to meet Maman in the courtyard.

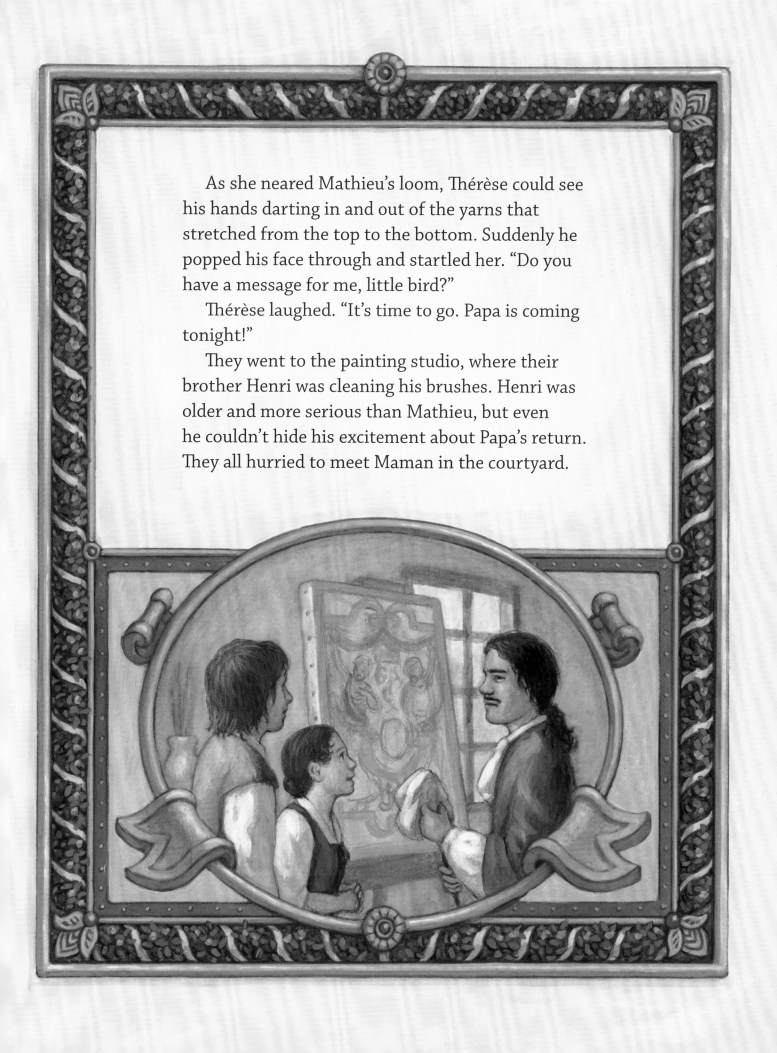

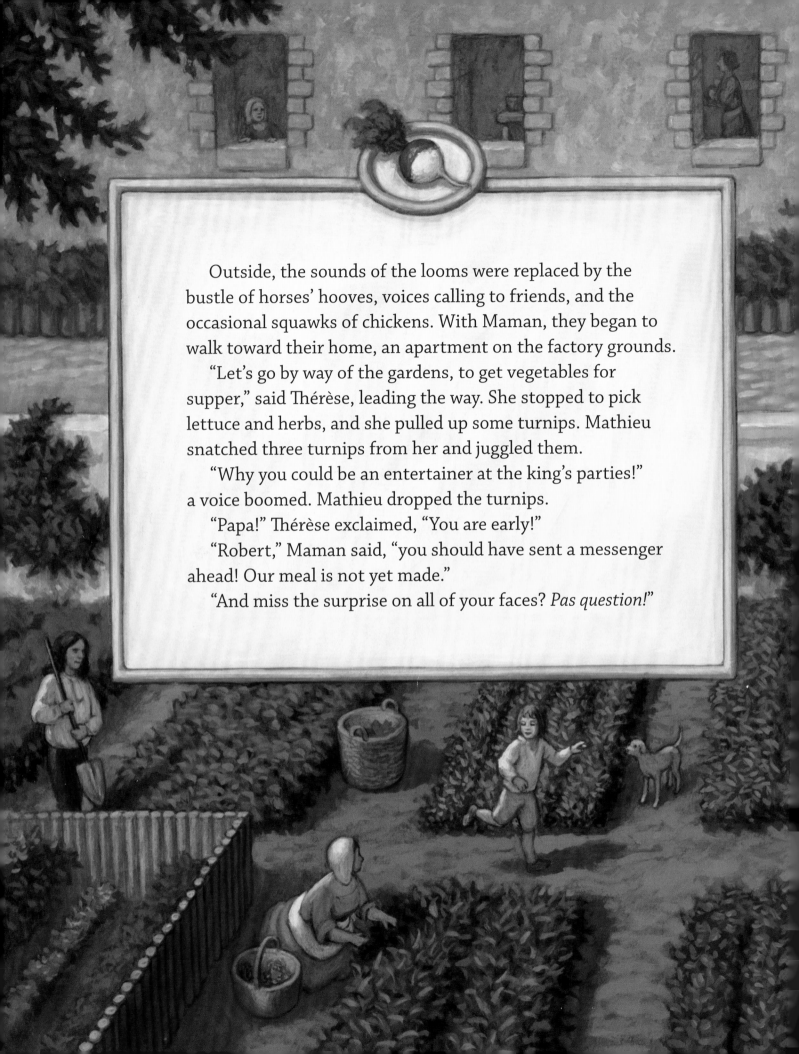

Outside, the sounds of the looms were replaced by the bustle of horses' hooves, voices calling to friends, and the occasional squawks of chickens. With Maman, they began to walk toward their home, an apartment on the factory grounds.

"Let's go by way of the gardens, to get vegetables for supper," said Thérèse, leading the way. She stopped to pick lettuce and herbs, and she pulled up some turnips. Mathieu snatched three turnips from her and juggled them.

"Why you could be an entertainer at the king's parties!" a voice boomed. Mathieu dropped the turnips.

"Papa!" Thérèse exclaimed, "You are early!"

"Robert," Maman said, "you should have sent a messenger ahead! Our meal is not yet made."

"And miss the surprise on all of your faces? *Pas question!*"

The family traded stories all during supper, until their bellies and hearts were full. Papa had been gone for two months and would leave again in two weeks. A magnificent painter, he followed King Louis XIV throughout France, painting scenes of battles, palaces, and nature.

"Thérèse, I have something for you, so that you won't forget me when I go away again." Papa winked.

Thérèse had never received a gift like this from Papa. What could it be? She untied the ribbon, and then she caught her breath. It was a painting of a palace in winter. The scene was lively with people, and around the edges were musical instruments, winter fruits, and birds like none she had ever seen. Papa told her the birds were part of the king's menagerie. Imagine having your own collection of exotic animals!

"Papa, thank you!" Thérèse managed at last. Papa squeezed her shoulders, and everyone crowded around to admire the painting.

"If you like the look of the king's palace, wait until you see the king himself!"

"What on earth do you mean, Papa?" Thérèse asked.

"King Louis is coming to visit!"

The whole family spoke at once. "Here?" "To the factory?" "When?!"

"One at a time, one at a time!" Papa chuckled.

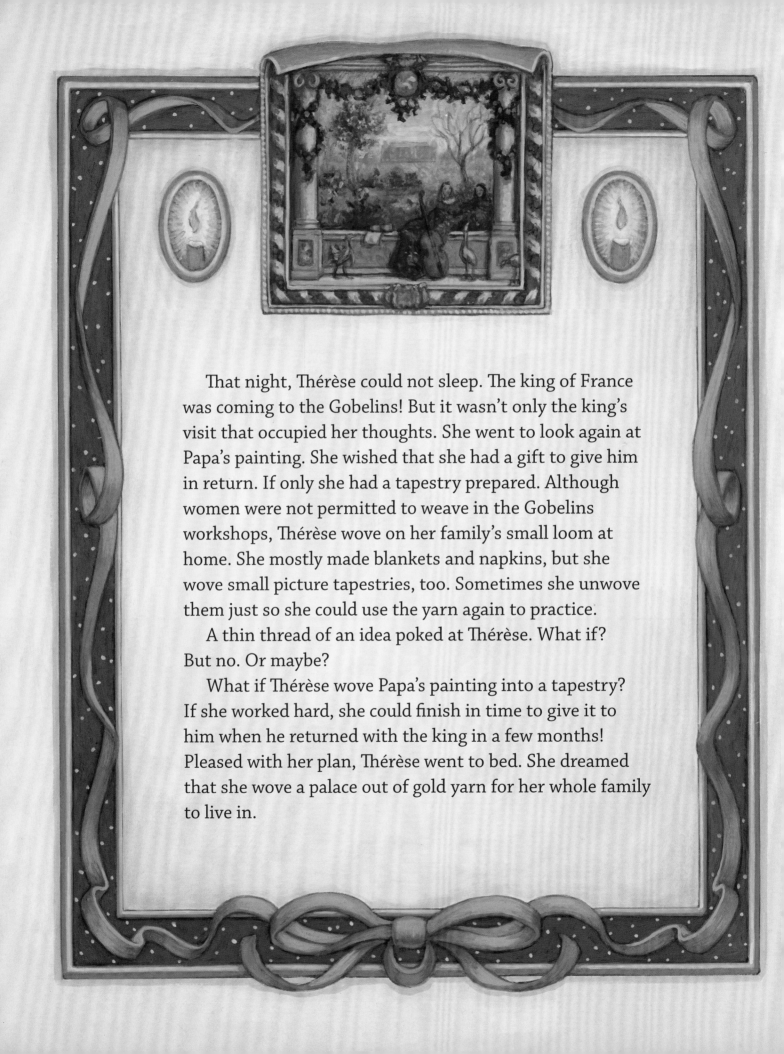

That night, Thérèse could not sleep. The king of France was coming to the Gobelins! But it wasn't only the king's visit that occupied her thoughts. She went to look again at Papa's painting. She wished that she had a gift to give him in return. If only she had a tapestry prepared. Although women were not permitted to weave in the Gobelins workshops, Thérèse wove on her family's small loom at home. She mostly made blankets and napkins, but she wove small picture tapestries, too. Sometimes she unwove them just so she could use the yarn again to practice.

A thin thread of an idea poked at Thérèse. What if? But no. Or maybe?

What if Thérèse wove Papa's painting into a tapestry? If she worked hard, she could finish in time to give it to him when he returned with the king in a few months! Pleased with her plan, Thérèse went to bed. She dreamed that she wove a palace out of gold yarn for her whole family to live in.

The next morning, Thérèse worked at her *dévidoir* alongside Maman. The wool she used had already been washed, combed, spun, and dyed. Today, she was creating a special yarn out of two different colors. Thérèse selected a green skein and a brown skein of wool. These she loaded onto her skein winders. With one hand she guided a thread from each skein to the empty spool. With the other hand she turned the crank that set the wheel spinning. She was careful to keep the tension of the threads steady as she plied them together to create a new yarn.

As she worked, Thérèse told her mother about her plan to surprise Papa with a tapestry. Maman sighed.

"That's a lovely idea, but are you sure you're ready to weave such a complicated design?"

"Maman, I can do it. I've been practicing."

Maman's worry lines softened. "In that case, I will do my best to help you."

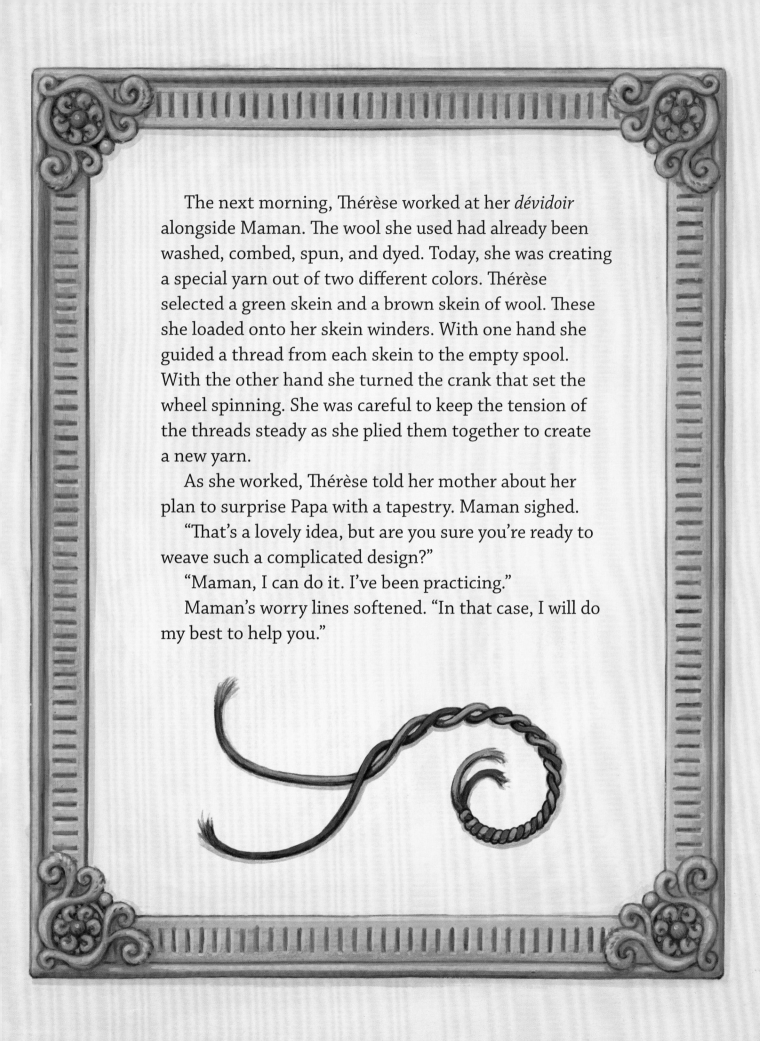

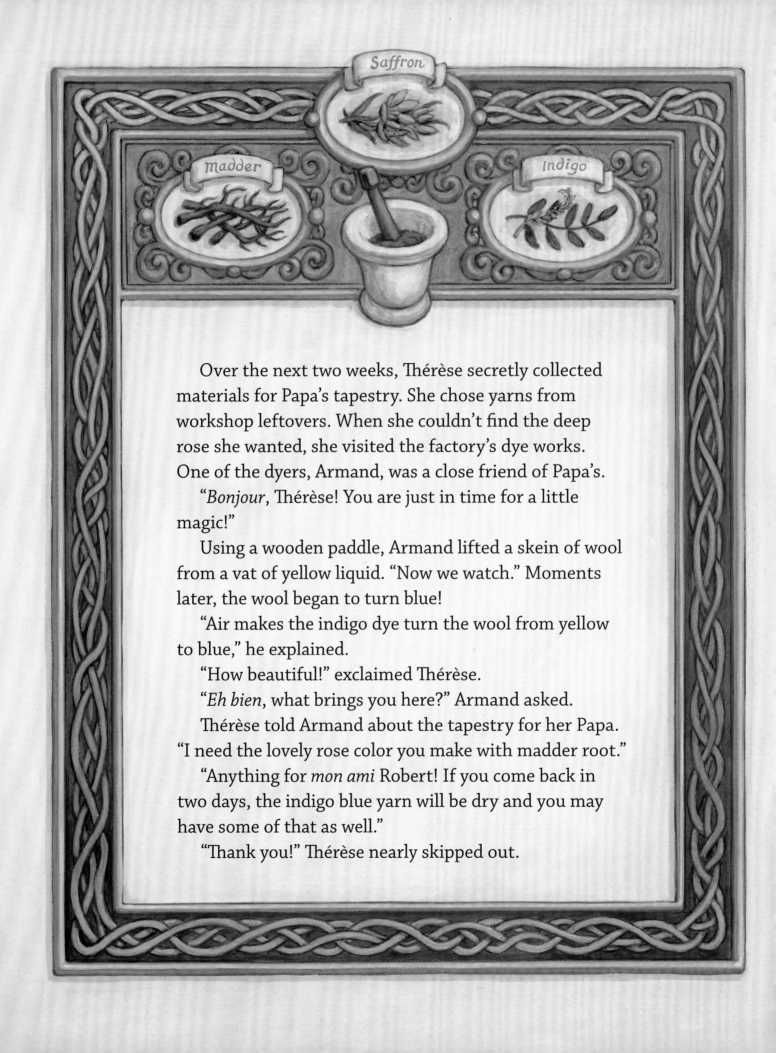

Over the next two weeks, Thérèse secretly collected materials for Papa's tapestry. She chose yarns from workshop leftovers. When she couldn't find the deep rose she wanted, she visited the factory's dye works. One of the dyers, Armand, was a close friend of Papa's.

"*Bonjour*, Thérèse! You are just in time for a little magic!"

Using a wooden paddle, Armand lifted a skein of wool from a vat of yellow liquid. "Now we watch." Moments later, the wool began to turn blue!

"Air makes the indigo dye turn the wool from yellow to blue," he explained.

"How beautiful!" exclaimed Thérèse.

"*Eh bien*, what brings you here?" Armand asked.

Thérèse told Armand about the tapestry for her Papa. "I need the lovely rose color you make with madder root."

"Anything for *mon ami* Robert! If you come back in two days, the indigo blue yarn will be dry and you may have some of that as well."

"Thank you!" Thérèse nearly skipped out.

There was something else Thérèse needed, and only one person she could ask … Henri. She walked to the painting studio to see him.

"To what do I owe this pleasure?" Henri grumbled. Thérèse explained her plan. Henri scoffed. "No girl can weave a masterful design like Papa's into a tapestry. You are wasting your time, but I can't let you waste mine."

Thérèse ignored her brother's biting remark. She hoped he would make a "cartoon," a larger version of Papa's painting that would be the same size as her tapestry. "Henri, please make me a simple copy? It does not need to be detailed or even in color." Henri scowled, but Thérèse persisted. "Please, it's for Papa." In the end, Henri agreed, but he made sure Thérèse knew just what a nuisance she was.

Two weeks passed quickly. It was difficult for Thérèse to say good-bye to Papa again. But it helped a little that, with him away, she could start working on his surprise.

First, she needed to warp the loom. To do this she took a single, long strand of undyed wool and looped it around the wooden beams at the top and bottom of the loom's frame. She laced this yarn under, over, and around the beams, again and again, until it was strung all across the loom. Using strong thread, she then secured the loops of yarn onto the beams. The yarn now cascaded into a fountain of evenly separated threads, called the warp.

The next day Thérèse inserted the cartoon Henri had made into the warp. She used black ink to trace the outlines of the design right onto the yarn. This created a kind of map for her to follow as she wove. Another day she organized her yarns, winding each color she would use onto its own bobbin. This yarn was called the weft yarn.

At last, Thérèse was ready to weave. She slipped her fingers through every other warp yarn and pulled them forward to pass a bobbin behind them. Then she reversed the position of the warp yarns and did the same thing in the opposite direction. Sometimes she used the pointed tip of her bobbin to push down the colored yarn, and every so often she stroked a small ivory comb down through the warp to tighten the weft.

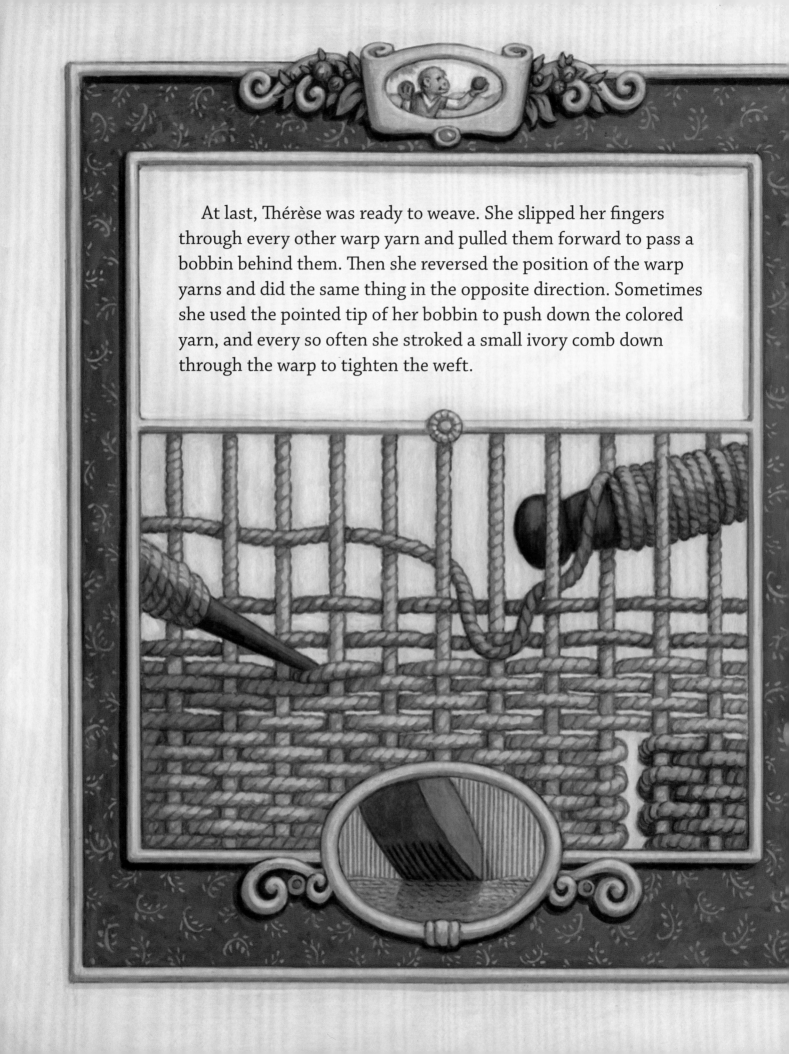

She used rose yarn for the carpet and indigo blue for bird feathers. When she finished with one color for the time being, she let that bobbin dangle and picked up the next color. When slits appeared between two colors, she stitched them up with a needle and thread.

Since Thérèse sat behind the loom, she used a mirror Maman had borrowed from the workshop to see the front of her tapestry. This made her feel like a true Gobelins weaver!

As she wove, Thérèse glanced often at Papa's painting. For while Henri's copy had allowed her to trace guiding lines onto the warp, she still needed the painting to see the colors and details. When she had woven the tapestry beyond a comfortable height, she rolled it onto the lower beam of the loom. As she did so, new warp came down from the top beam and the whole process began anew.

Slowly, slowly, Papa's painting came to life in Thérèse's tapestry. Maman was so impressed that she told Thérèse not to worry about her chores.

"*Mais* Maman ...," Thérèse began to object.

"Hush now, Thérèse. I want you to finish your tapestry well. I can take over your most important tasks for now, and the rest can wait."

With whole days to weave, Thérèse made faster progress. Eventually she completed everything but the top border. For that she wanted something special.

Thérèse went to the metalsmith's workshop, where she found Thomas, the smith, making wire by pulling a strand of silver through smaller and smaller holes.

"May I help you?" he asked.

"I wonder if you could spare any silver thread. I don't need much."

"With the king coming, I can give silver thread only to those working on a piece for his viewing."

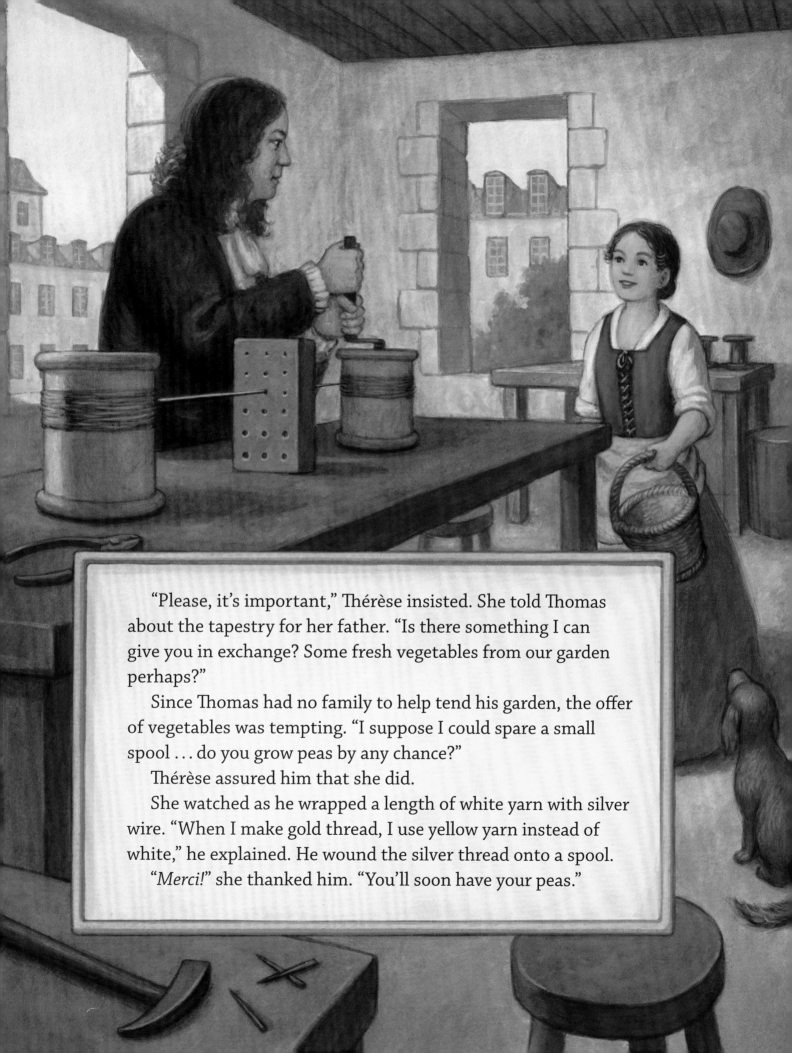

"Please, it's important," Thérèse insisted. She told Thomas about the tapestry for her father. "Is there something I can give you in exchange? Some fresh vegetables from our garden perhaps?"

Since Thomas had no family to help tend his garden, the offer of vegetables was tempting. "I suppose I could spare a small spool ... do you grow peas by any chance?"

Thérèse assured him that she did.

She watched as he wrapped a length of white yarn with silver wire. "When I make gold thread, I use yellow yarn instead of white," he explained. He wound the silver thread onto a spool.

"*Merci!*" she thanked him. "You'll soon have your peas."

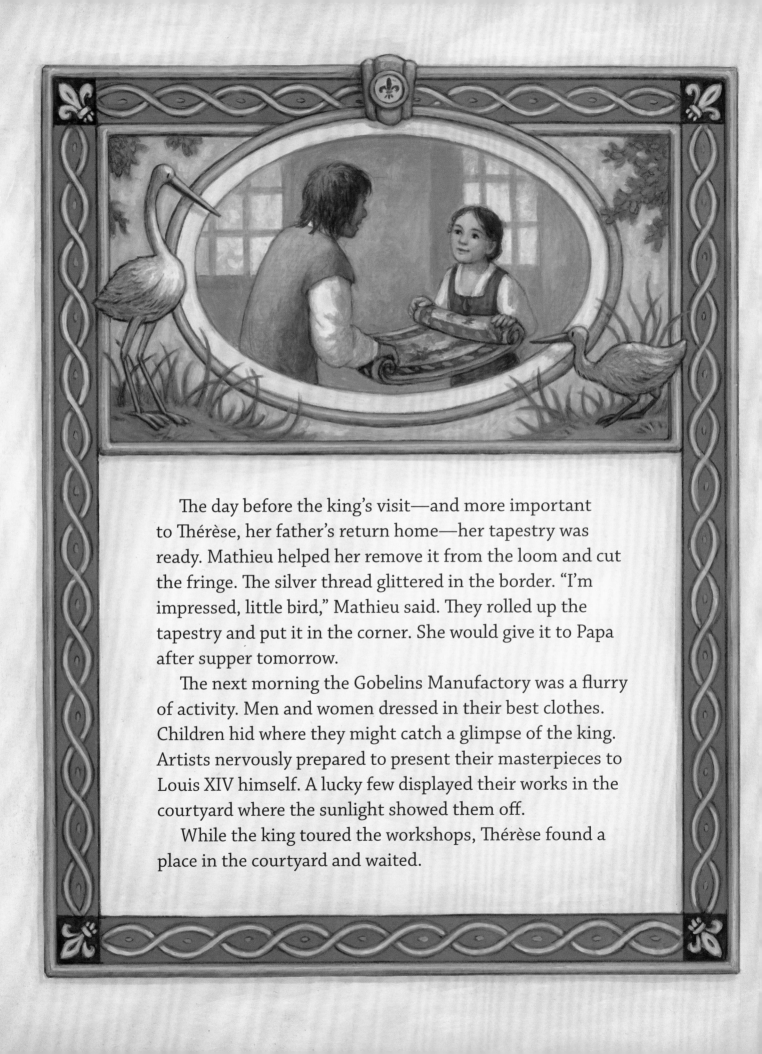

The day before the king's visit—and more important to Thérèse, her father's return home—her tapestry was ready. Mathieu helped her remove it from the loom and cut the fringe. The silver thread glittered in the border. "I'm impressed, little bird," Mathieu said. They rolled up the tapestry and put it in the corner. She would give it to Papa after supper tomorrow.

The next morning the Gobelins Manufactory was a flurry of activity. Men and women dressed in their best clothes. Children hid where they might catch a glimpse of the king. Artists nervously prepared to present their masterpieces to Louis XIV himself. A lucky few displayed their works in the courtyard where the sunlight showed them off.

While the king toured the workshops, Thérèse found a place in the courtyard and waited.

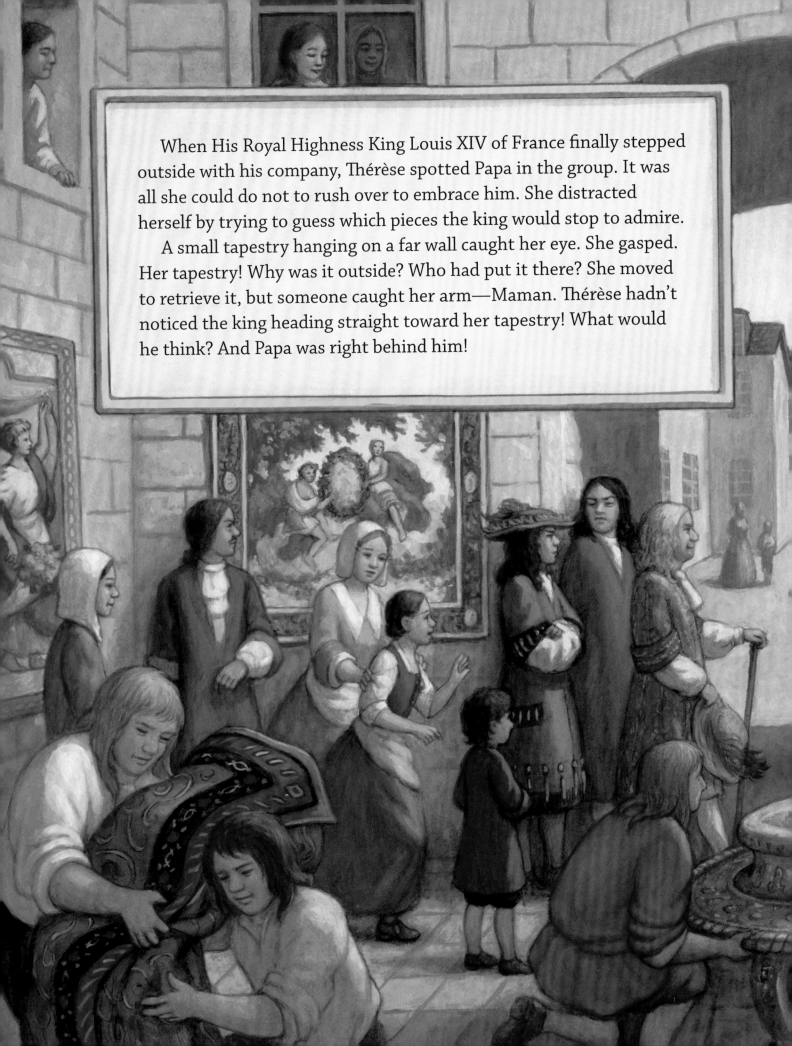

When His Royal Highness King Louis XIV of France finally stepped outside with his company, Thérèse spotted Papa in the group. It was all she could do not to rush over to embrace him. She distracted herself by trying to guess which pieces the king would stop to admire.

A small tapestry hanging on a far wall caught her eye. She gasped. Her tapestry! Why was it outside? Who had put it there? She moved to retrieve it, but someone caught her arm—Maman. Thérèse hadn't noticed the king heading straight toward her tapestry! What would he think? And Papa was right behind him!

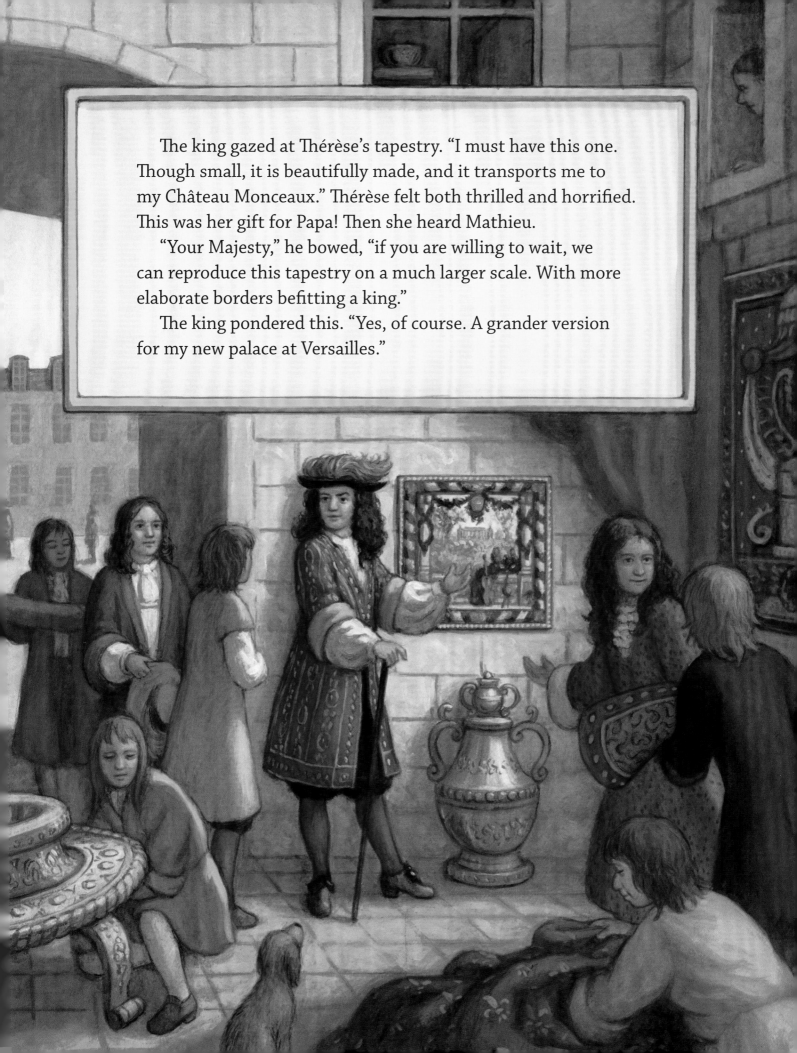

The king gazed at Thérèse's tapestry. "I must have this one. Though small, it is beautifully made, and it transports me to my Château Monceaux." Thérèse felt both thrilled and horrified. This was her gift for Papa! Then she heard Mathieu.

"Your Majesty," he bowed, "if you are willing to wait, we can reproduce this tapestry on a much larger scale. With more elaborate borders befitting a king."

The king pondered this. "Yes, of course. A grander version for my new palace at Versailles."

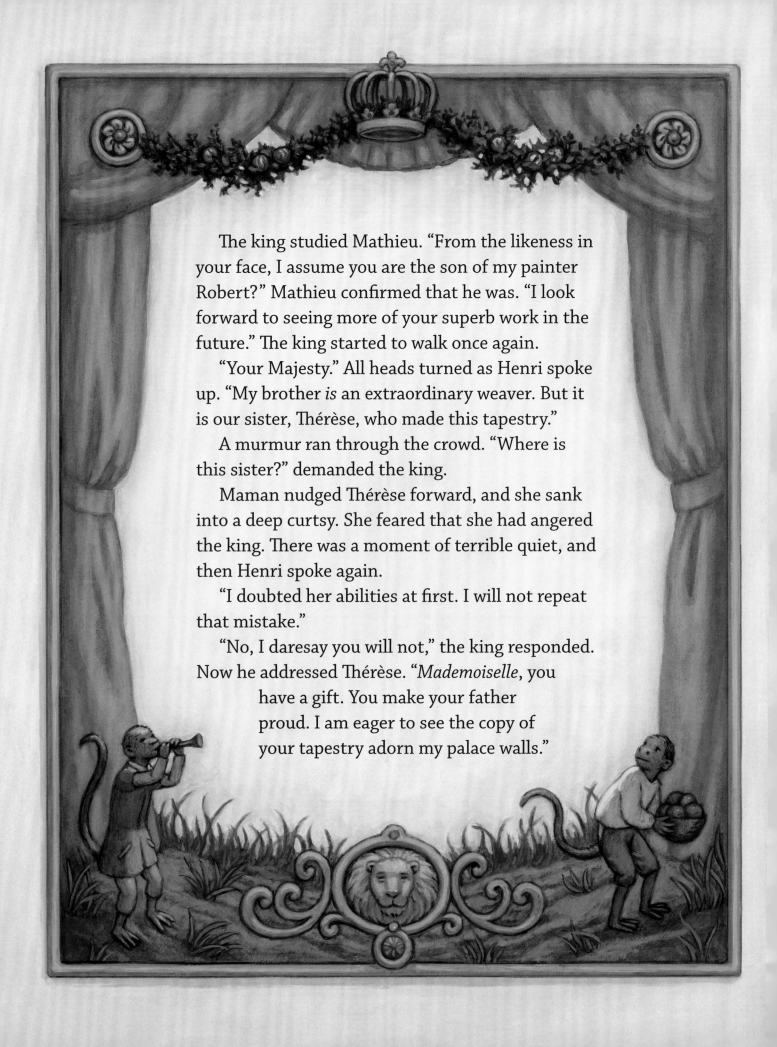

The king studied Mathieu. "From the likeness in your face, I assume you are the son of my painter Robert?" Mathieu confirmed that he was. "I look forward to seeing more of your superb work in the future." The king started to walk once again.

"Your Majesty." All heads turned as Henri spoke up. "My brother *is* an extraordinary weaver. But it is our sister, Thérèse, who made this tapestry."

A murmur ran through the crowd. "Where is this sister?" demanded the king.

Maman nudged Thérèse forward, and she sank into a deep curtsy. She feared that she had angered the king. There was a moment of terrible quiet, and then Henri spoke again.

"I doubted her abilities at first. I will not repeat that mistake."

"No, I daresay you will not," the king responded. Now he addressed Thérèse. "*Mademoiselle*, you have a gift. You make your father proud. I am eager to see the copy of your tapestry adorn my palace walls."

Papa returned home later with a twinkle in his eye. "What an impression my family has made! And Thérèse, I have never received a more wonderful gift. Thank you, *ma chère enfant*." Papa kissed Thérèse's cheeks.

"I'm very glad you like it, Papa. But I still don't understand how my tapestry ended up in the courtyard."

"That was my doing," said Henri, to everyone's surprise. "I saw it waiting in the corner, and it was so expertly woven that I decided to put it on display so all could view it … and see how wrong I had been about you, Thérèse."

Thérèse was speechless as Henri gave her a rare smile.

As usual, Mathieu was happy to fill the silence. "Then Henri, I presume you will make us the larger cartoon for the king's tapestry? And, of course, Thérèse will have to help me with the weaving."

Thérèse's heart swelled. She would weave in the royal workshop, for the king! Her dream, as lofty as the great Gobelins looms, was about to come true.

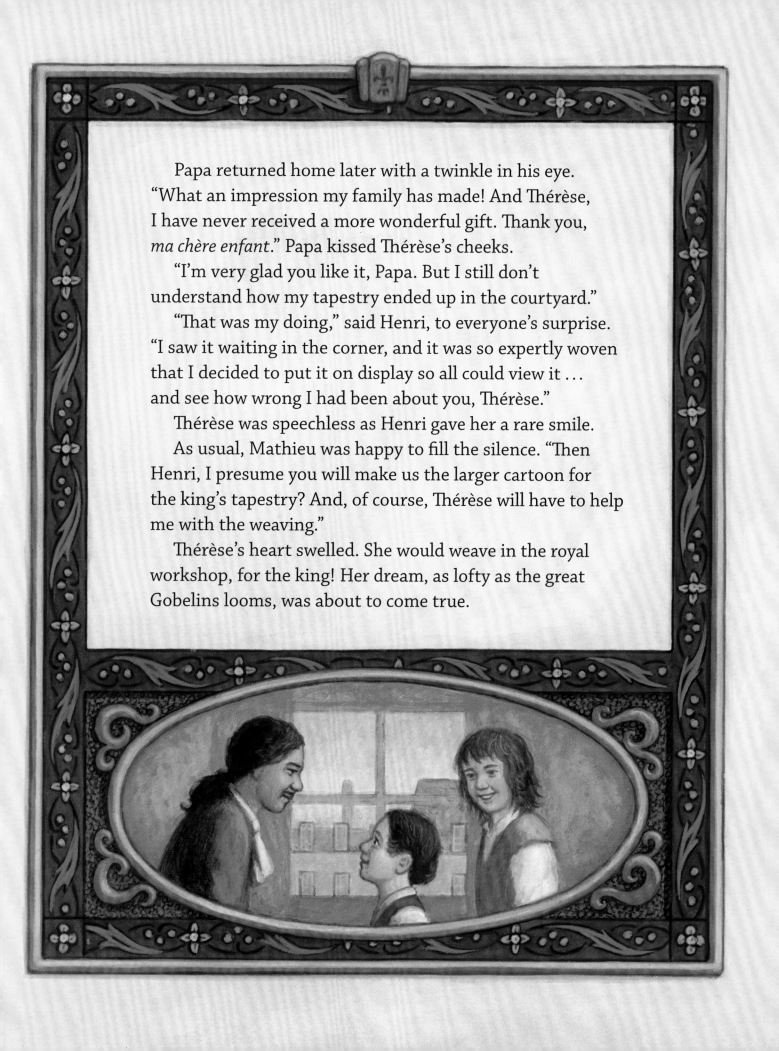

Note to the Reader

THÉRÈSE'S STORY was inspired by real tapestries, real people, and a real place.

The tapestry Thérèse weaves resembles a real tapestry called the *Château of Monceaux / Month of December*. It is part of a series that depicts King Louis XIV's royal residences and also the months of the year. This tapestry shows the king leading a hunting party on the grounds of his château. On the right, two pages in uniform display a carpet, and musical instruments rest along a wall. The exotic birds (which Thérèse notices in the story) are a moorhen, crane, and bustard. Multiple versions of this tapestry were produced in different sizes, and some can be viewed in museums today. The large version shown on the last page of the story is based on a real tapestry in the collection of the Mobilier National, Paris. It is nearly thirteen feet high and twenty feet long!

Although Thérèse herself is fictional, King Louis XIV was a real king who ruled France from 1643 to 1715. He was an important patron of the arts. One of his favorite subjects was himself! He ordered a series of fourteen tapestries called *The Story of the King* to show his life and achievements. One depicts his visit to the Gobelins Manufactory on October 15, 1667. It captures the flurry of excitement that Thérèse experiences in the story.

The character of Thérèse's father is based on a real painter named Adam-François van der Meulen. He specialized in battle scenes and traveled with King Louis XIV on his military campaigns. He helped paint the design for the *Château of Monceaux / Month of December*. While Thérèse's Papa is French, Van der Meulen was one of many Flemish artists who moved to France to be part of the vibrant art scene at the court of Louis XIV.

The Gobelins Manufactory where Thérèse lives is a real place that you can visit today. It was founded on the site of an old dye and, later, tapestry workshop in Paris. In the 1660s King Louis XIV's finance minister turned the factory into a place where artists and artisans fashioned exquisite furnishings and decorations for His Majesty's royal dwellings. Europe's finest painters, sculptors, goldsmiths, cabinetmakers, and metalworkers, along with dyers and weavers, came here to work. Today at the Gobelins Manufactory you can still see master weavers at fifteen great looms.

The Gobelins tapestries are world famous, and numerous artists and weavers were involved in the creation of each one. For example, twelve painters produced the cartoons for the *Château of Monceaux / Month of December*. Each specialized in something different, such as people, flowers and fruit, animals and birds, or landscapes. Weavers worked together, too, often sitting side-by-side at a single loom in one of the weaving workshops. We know the details of the weaving process from descriptions and illustrations in a famous encyclopedia published in the eighteenth century by Denis Diderot and Jean le Rond d'Alembert.

While there were metalworkers and metal shops at the Gobelins, we do not know whether silver thread was made on site. Gold and silver thread were more likely purchased elsewhere. We do know that the king supplied all materials that the artists needed, but that he subtracted the costs of those materials from the pieces he purchased.

Weavers and their families lived in housing on the Gobelins property. They had gardens to grow their own vegetables, just like Thérèse's family. The same garden plots belonged to the weavers' families and their descendants for as long as three hundred years! Although women and children lived and worked at the Gobelins, women were not trained as weavers. But this does not mean that women and girls did not weave elsewhere and for other purposes. In fact, women and girls have a long history with textiles and weaving. And Thérèse would be pleased to know that some of the master weavers at the Gobelins today are women!

For more information and activities related to
Thérèse Makes a Tapestry, visit **www.getty.edu/education/therese**

Glossary

bobbin. A short wooden peg, sometimes with a pointed end, around which yarn is wound.

cartoon. A drawing or painting that weavers use as a guide for making a tapestry.

dévidoir. A contraption that looks like a spinning wheel and can be used to wind yarn onto bobbins or spools. It can also be used to twist together two or more yarns of different colors into one yarn of blended colors.

dye. A substance that can be dissolved in liquid and used to give color to fabric or yarn. In Thérèse's time, dyes were natural and came from all sorts of plants and some animals such as insects and mollusks.

loom. A device used for weaving that holds warp yarns in place. The loom Thérèse uses is called a high-warp loom, or vertical loom. It is used for tapestries and is wider than other types of looms.

manufactory. A place where something is manufactured or made. The shorter version of this word, "factory," is more common today.

menagerie. A collection of exotic animals intended for display.

skein. A very long piece of yarn that is loosely coiled.

spool. A revolving wooden rod around which yarn is wound.

tapestry. A woven picture that hangs on a wall. King Louis XIV's tapestries were made of wool, silk, and gilded thread. Not only symbols of great wealth, tapestries also kept rooms warmer during cold months.

warp. The group of undyed yarns that run vertically (up and down) on a high-warp loom. Horizontal (side-to-side) weft yarns are passed through the warp to create the woven tapestry.

weave. The process of interlacing yarns to create a fabric.

weft. The group of colorful yarns that run horizontally (from side to side) across the vertical warp yarns.

yarn. A material such as wool, silk, or cotton that has been twisted or spun into a strand and is used to create cloth.

French Words and Phrases

bonjour (BONE-joor) – hello

dévidoir (DAY-vee-dwahr) – *see glossary at left*

eh bien (ai BEE-en) – well

ma chère enfant (mah share on-font) – my dear child

mademoiselle (ma-dem-was-elle) – Miss; young lady

mais (may) – but

Maman (ma-MA) – Mama

merci (mare-SEE) – thank you

mon ami (mone ah-mee) – my friend

pas question (pah KEST-ee-ohn) – out of the question

Thérèse (teh-REZ)

This *Château of Monceaux / Month of December* tapestry was created at the Gobelins Manufactory before 1712. It is now in the collection of the J. Paul Getty Museum in Los Angeles.

Metalsmith's Workshop

MAP
of
the
GOBELINS
MANUFACTORY

© 2015 J. Paul Getty Trust
Illustrations © Renée Graef

**Published by the J. Paul Getty Museum,
Los Angeles**
Getty Publications
1200 Getty Center Drive, Suite 500
Los Angeles, California 90049–1682
www.getty.edu/publications

Elizabeth S. G. Nicholson, *Project Editor*
Charissa Bremer-David, *Curatorial Adviser*
Kimberly Chrisman-Campbell, *Costume Consultant*
Ann Grogg, *Copyeditor*
Jim Drobka, *Designer*
Elizabeth Kahn, *Production*
Johana Herrera, *Imaging Technician*

Distributed in the United States and Canada
by the University of Chicago Press
Distributed outside the United States and Canada
by Yale University Press, London

Printed and bound by Tien Wah Press, Malaysia (59001)
First printing by the J. Paul Getty Museum (14121)

Library of Congress Cataloging-in-Publication Data
Hinrichs, Alexandra S. D., 1984– author.
  Thérèse makes a tapestry / written by Alexandra S. D.
Hinrichs ; illustrated by Renée Graef.
    pages cm
  ISBN 978-1-60606-473-3 (hardcover)
  [1. Tapestry—Fiction. 2. Weaving—Fiction.] I. Graef,
Renée, illustrator. II. Title.
  PZ7.1.H57Th 2015
  [E]—dc23
                    2015024052

The artist would like to thank the models for the illustrations:
Ella Knox, Arika Knox, Ricky Knox, Maxfield Laughner,
Maggie Laughner, and Bruce Malm.